The Day-Off Machine

BY JOHN HIMMELMAN

Silver Press

To Kristelle, Love Uncle John.
—J.H.

Library of Congress Cataloging-in-Publication Data

Himmelman, John.
   The day-off machine / by John Himmelman.
   p. cm.—(The Fix-it family)
   Summary: Graham's new invention combines with a big snowfall to
force his busy beaver family to take a day off from their chores.
   [1. Beavers—Fiction. 2. Inventors—Fiction. 3. Family life—
Fiction. 4. Snow—Fiction.] I. Title. II. Series: Himmelman,
John, Fix-it family.
PZ7.H5686Day 1990
[E]—dc20   90-31337
ISBN 0-671-69635-1 (lib. bdg.)   CIP
ISBN 0-671-69639-4 (pbk.)   AC

Produced by Small Packages, Inc.
Copyright © 1990 by Small Packages, Inc. and John Himmelman.
Published by Silver Press, a division of
Silver Burdett Press, Inc.
Simon & Schuster, Inc.,
Prentice Hall Bldg., Englewood Cliffs, NJ 07632.
Printed in the United States of America.
10 9 8 7 6 5 4 3 2 1

The Fix-It Family

Orville and Willa Wright

own a fix-it shop.

If something is broken,

they will repair it.

They can fix anything!

They are also inventors.

And their children—

Alexander, Graham, and Belle—

like inventing things, too.

CHAPTER ONE
Work, Work, Work

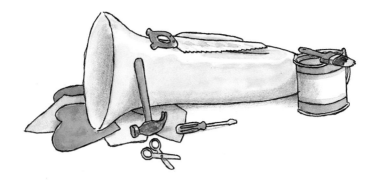

Graham loved winter.

It meant holidays and snow.

It meant time off

to have fun with his family.

But this winter,

Orville was extra busy

in the fix-it shop.

"Poor Dad," thought Graham.

"He has not had a day off in weeks.

But tomorrow is Saturday.

Maybe he will take the day off."

It began to snow.

Graham hurried to the fix-it shop.

"It's snowing!" he told his father.

"Hooray!" shouted Orville.

"I love the snow."

"Can you play outside

with us tomorrow?" asked Graham.

"I wish I could," said Orville.

"But I have to fix

Greg Gopher's easy chair.

And Mrs. Mousello wants

a new cheese maker."

He looked sad.

"Maybe your mother

will play with you," he said.

Graham found his mother in the kitchen.

She was painting the walls.

"It's snowing!" he told her.

"That is good," she said.

"Maybe your father will take

the day off tomorrow."

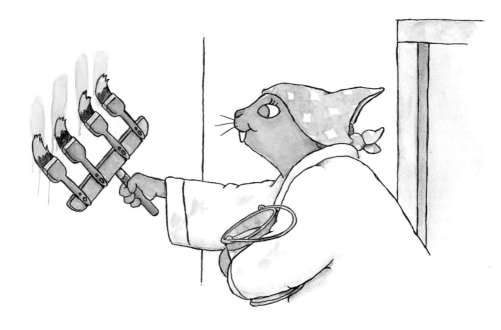

"He is too busy," said Graham.

"He said to ask you."

"I am busy, too," said Willa.

"Why don't you ask Alexander."

Alexander was practicing his tuba.

"It's snowing," said Graham.

"Will you play outside
with me tomorrow?"

"Is Dad taking the day off?"
asked Alexander.

"No," Graham said sadly.

"Then I will not take

a day off either," said Alexander.

"I should practice my tuba."

Graham went to Belle's room.

She was cutting out great big shapes.

"It's snowing," Graham told her.

"Do you want to play outside tomorrow?"

"With Dad, too?" asked Belle.

"No," said Graham.

"He has too much work to do."

"Then so do I," said Belle.

"This is not good," thought Graham.

"I will have to invent a way

to give Dad a day off."

He went outside

and climbed onto the slide.

It was a good place to think.

Finally he had an idea.

"This slide could be
part of my invention," he said.

"But it will need some changes."

First he got the snow shovel

and put it in the shop.

Then he went to work.

By dinnertime he was finished.

He pushed the slide

in front of the shop door.

And later that night,

while everyone slept,

Graham's invention went to work.

CHAPTER TWO
The Day-Off Machine

The next day,

Graham woke up early.

He looked out the window.

"Wake up, wake up!" he shouted.

Everyone came running.

"Look at all the snow,"

said Alexander.

"Look at the shop!" said Belle.

Graham's slide sat

in front of the fix-it shop.

It was buried in snow.

"What is that?" asked Belle.

"It is my invention," said Graham.

"Your invention has piled snow
in front of the door," said Orville.

"Yes," said Graham.

"And the snow shovel is in the shop."

Orville tried to look sad.

But he could not help smiling.

"I guess I cannot go to work,"

he said.

"No, you cannot," said Graham.

"That is why my invention is called

the Day-Off Machine."

Orville gave Graham a big hug.

"You are a very good inventor,"

he said.

"I will take the day off, too,"
said Belle.

"Me, too," said Alexander.

"I guess the kitchen can wait,"
said Willa.

So after breakfast,

the whole family went outside.

They had snowball fights.

They went sledding down the big hill.

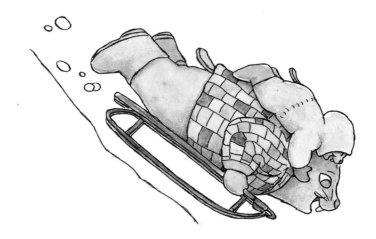

They skated on the frozen lake.

"Let's build a snowman!" said Willa.

"Let's build a snow FAMILY,"
said Graham.

When they finished,

they were covered with snow.

And it looked as if

there were *two* beaver families

taking the day off.

Soon it was time for supper.

"This was a fun day," said Orville.

"I love the snow."

"We know," said his family.

Orville hung his coat in the closet.

At the back of the closet

he found an old snow shovel.

"It looks as if tomorrow

will not be a fun day for me,"

he said.

"I really should dig out the shop

and go back to work."

Orville did not look happy anymore.

His family wanted him to feel better.

"That is okay," said Willa.

"Tomorrow I should paint the kitchen."

"Yes, and I should practice my tuba,"

said Alexander.

"And I should make more shapes,"

said Belle.

"It looks as if we will need

another Day-Off Machine,"

thought Graham.

"I will be busy, also," he said.

"In fact, I have so much to do,

I will have to start tonight!"

CHAPTER THREE
The Very Busy Snowmen

Graham rushed through his supper.

"Can I go outside?" he asked.

"Yes, you may," said Willa.

"But don't you want to play

a board game with us?"

"No thanks," said Graham.

"I will be too busy for games."

He put on his coat.

Then he grabbed two flashlights.

"Why do you need two flashlights?"

asked Orville.

"It is very dark outside,"

said Graham.

"I need one light for each eye."

Orville laughed.

Graham ran outside.

A few minutes later,

Graham ran back inside.

"Where is the garden hose?" he asked.

"It is in the garage," said Willa.

"But why do you need a hose?"

Graham did not answer.

He was already back outside.

While the others played their game,

Graham ran in and out of the house.

"What is Graham doing?" asked Belle.

"I wish I knew," said Willa.

Just then, Graham ran into the room.

"Come quick!" he shouted.

"I heard a funny noise outside!"

He ran back out.

The others hurried after him.

"Hey, look at the snowmen!"

said Alexander.

Belle's snowman was holding her

paper and scissors.

Alexander's snowman
was wearing his tuba.
Willa's snowman held all of
her paintbrushes.
And Orville's snowman
held the old snow shovel.

Graham was hiding behind

his snowman.

He turned on a switch.

His snowman's eyes lit up!

Then he spoke through
the end of the hose.
The sound came out of
his snowman's mouth!
"I am Graham's snowman," he said.
"My snowman family
needs to borrow your things."

"But what about our work?"

asked Willa.

"It will have to wait,"

said the snowman.

"Tomorrow is a busy day

for snowmen.

But it is a day off

for beaver families."

Orville winked at Willa.

"We cannot argue with a snowman,"

he said.

"No, you cannot," said the snowman.

"And one more thing.

When you go inside,

give that nice boy Graham

a big cup of hot cocoa."

"Whatever you say,"

Willa said with a laugh.

She and the others went inside.

Soon Graham joined them.

And they all sat around the table
and drank hot cocoa.
Tomorrow would be
another fun day.

The End